MOMOTARO

Hand-painted paper: CLAIRE MAZIARCZYK

Library of Congress number: 89-3579

Library of Congress Cataloging in Publication Data

Motomora, Mitchell.
   Momotaro / Mitchell Motomora; illustrated by Kyuzo Tsugami.

   (Real readers)
   Summary: Found floating on the river inside a peach by an old couple, Momotaro
grows up and fights the terrible demons who have terrorized the village for years.
   [1. Folklore—Japan.] I. Tsugami, Kyuzo, ill. II. Title. III. Series.
PZ8.1.M85Mo 1989   398.2′1′0952—dc19 [E]   89-3579
ISBN: 0-8172-3513-2

1 2 3 4 5 6 7 8 9 0   93 92 91 90 89

REAL READERS

MOMOTARO

by Mitchell Motomora • illustrated by Kyuzo Tsugami

Raintree Publishers
Milwaukee

One day, a woman went down to the water to do her wash. When she got there, she saw something in the water. It was shaped like a ball. But it wasn't a ball. It was a peach. And it was as big as her wash tub!

The woman wanted the peach. But she could not reach it. How could she get it?

How she wished she could get that peach! She was so sad that she sang a song:

"Big peach, big peach
Come close, so I can reach."

And odd as it may seem, the peach did just as the woman asked!

She put the peach on top of her wash tub, and took it home to show her husband.

Her husband was very pleased with the peach. "I will cut this peach in two," he said. "Then we will have a fine meal."

But just as he was about to cut into the peach, someone called out, "Stop! Don't cut into my peach! I will come out."

KAPOP, KATHUMP, KABOOM!

The peach broke, and out jumped
a little boy.

"Can I be your little boy?" the peach
boy asked.

"Yes," said the woman.

"Yes," said the man.

They named the boy Momotaro. In
Japanese, that means "peach boy".

Momotaro and his mother and father led a happy life. Then, when Momotaro was 15, some ogres came to his city.

CRASH, STOMP, GRAB!

The ogres laughed mean laughs. They pushed. They broke things. They took all the money Momotaro's mother and father had.

And then they went back home to Ogre Island.

Momotaro wanted to go bring back the things the orges took. But his mother and father did not want him to go.

"But the ogres live way out at sea, on Ogre Island!" said his mother and father.

But Momotaro still wanted to go. At last his mother and father said that he could.

The next day, Momotaro's mother gave him a bag with 3 cakes in it, and he set off for Ogre Island.

So Momotaro walked to the sea. On the way, he saw a dog. The dog looked so hungry that Momotaro gave it one of his cakes.

"Thank you," said the dog. "Where are you going with that bag of cakes?"

"I am going to Ogre Island," said Momotaro. "I want to bring back all the things the ogres took."

"Grrr! Grrr!" said the dog. "Let me come, too. I want to help."

So Momotaro and the dog walked to the
sea. On the way, they saw a monkey.
The monkey looked so hungry that
Momotaro gave it one of his cakes.

"Thank you," said the monkey. "Where
are you going with that bag of cakes?"

"I am going to Ogre Island," said
Momotaro. "I want to bring back all the
things the ogres took."

"Chee! Chee!" said the monkey. "Let
me come, too. I want to help."

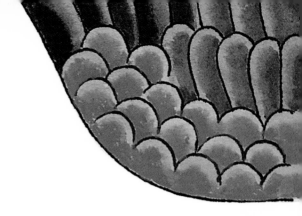

So Momotaro, the dog, and the monkey walked to the sea. On the way, they saw a bird. The bird looked so hungry that Momotaro gave it his last cake.

"Thank you," said the bird. "Where are you going with that bag of cakes?"

"I am going to Ogre Island," said Momotaro. "I want to bring back all the things the ogres took."

"Twee! Twee!" said the bird. "Let me come, too. I want to help."

So Momotaro, the dog, the monkey,
and the bird all walked to the sea.
Then they got in a boat and sailed
to Ogre Island.

At first, all they could see was fog all
around Ogre Island. Then they saw that
the ogres had a big city and the city
had big walls all around it.

"Bird," Momotaro said, "you can
fly up over the walls. Go into the city
and open the gate. Then we
can all get in."

The bird did as Momotaro said. Soon all
the friends were in the city. Momotaro
led them to the home of the Ogre King.

"I am Momotaro, the peach boy,"
Momotaro said. "And I want you to give
back all the things you took!"

"Ha, ha, ha," laughed the Ogre King.
"How can a little peach boy make me
give back all the things I took?"

All the other ogres laughed, too.

"Twee! Twee! Don't laugh at Momotaro!"
said the bird.

"Chee! Chee! Don't laugh at Momotaro!"
said the monkey.

"Grrr! Grrr! Don't laugh at Momotaro!"
said the dog.

But the Ogre King and all the other
ogres still laughed.

The animals got so mad that they all jumped on the Ogre King at the same time. He got scared. He was not used to being jumped on. He started to yell, "Help! Help!"

But the other ogres did not come to help him. They all ran away. They did not want the animals to jump on them!

"Ow!" yelled the Ogre King. "Stop! You can have all your things back. Take my ring, too."

So, Momotaro and his friends went home. They gave back all the things that the ogres had taken.

Momotaro asked his father to sell the Ogre King's ring. Then the peach boy used the money to get a fine, new home. There, Momotaro, his mother, his father, and his 3 good friends all lived long and happy lives.

Sharing the Joy of Reading

Beginning readers enjoy reading books on their own. Reading a book is a worthwhile activity in and of itself for a young reader. However, a child's reading can be even more rewarding if it is shared. This sharing can enhance your child's appreciation—both of the book and of his or her own abilities.

Now that your child has read **Momotaro**, you can help extend your child's reading experience by encouraging him or her to:

- Retell the story or key concepts presented in this story in his or her own words. The retelling can be oral or written.

- Create a picture of a favorite character, event, or concept from this book.

- Express his or her own ideas and feelings about the characters in this book and other things the characters might do.

Here is a special activity that you and your child can do together to further extend your child's appreciation of this book: This book is an example of a Japanese folktale. You can share other folktales from Japan or other countries with your child. Select a folktale you may have in a book at home or select a folktale from the library to read aloud to your child. Your child can then read aloud to you using this book, **Momotaro**, or retell the story for you using his or her own words.